For Winifred Clarke
with thanks

M.M.

First published 1992
by Walker Books Ltd, 87 Vauxhall Walk
London SE11 5HJ

Text © 1992 Michelle Magorian
Illustrations © 1992 Jan Ormerod

First printed 1992
Printed and bound in Hong Kong by
South China Printing Co. (1988) Ltd

British Library Cataloguing in Publication Data
Magorian, Michelle
Jump.
I.Title II. Ormerod, Jan
823'.914 [J]

ISBN 0-7445-2112-2

JUMP!

Written by Michelle Magorian

Illustrated by Jan Ormerod

WALKER BOOKS
LONDON

Every Saturday morning, Steven sat with his father and watched his older sister, Theresa, at her ballet class. There were three boys in the class – Michael, Joe and Barry. Steven longed to join them. When the boys and girls jumped, Steven leaned forward and pretended he was jumping too. After the class he danced with Theresa all the way home.

One day, when the boys and girls were bending their knees at the barre, Steven overheard the teacher saying, "Remember, class, the deeper you can plié, the higher you will be able to jump." Steven watched even more closely. Jumping was the thing he liked doing best.

As soon as
he was
home he
practised.

In
the hall.

In the
kitchen.

"What are you doing, Steven?"
asked his mother.
"I'm pliéing like Theresa does in
dance classes."
"You don't want to do that," she said.
Steven was puzzled. I do, he thought.
"Mum, can I go to dance classes?"
His mother's mouth opened wide.
"Certainly not. Real boys
don't go to dance
classes."

By the bath.

The following Saturday, after the
class had done their bows and curtsies,
Steven walked over to where the boys
were putting on their tracksuits.

He squeezed Michael's arm, he touched
Joe's back and he gave Barry's hair a tug.
"What are you doing?" they asked.
"I'm seeing if you're real," said Steven.
"Well, we are," they said.

"They are real, Mum," he told his mother.
"You can play basketball," she said, looking
up from the television, "and that's that."
"What's basketball?"
"A game, a tough game, with a ball," she
said, and pointed at the screen. "Look."

"They're jumping!" he exclaimed.
"Yes," said his mum, "as high as they can."
"Good," said Steven. "Can I play it today?"
"We don't have a ball or a net, and you need somewhere to play it," she said.
"You'll have to grow a bit too."

"Oh," Steven sighed, disappointed. He raced into his and Theresa's bedroom and pliéd and leapt and flung his arms as wildly as he could until he felt better.

At the next class, when
the boys were jumping, Steven
couldn't sit still any longer.
He ran across the floor.
His father tried to pull him away.
"Let him stay," said the teacher.
"He's good."
After the jumps the teacher said,
"Show me what else you
can do, Steven."
So he did.

The children clapped.
"Would you like to be in
the show this year?" the
teacher asked.
"Will you teach me a basketball
dance?" asked Steven.
The teacher laughed.
"Well," she said, "I'll see."

On the night of the show,
Steven's mum and dad sat in the audience.
"Where's Steven?" his mum asked.
"He's here," said Steven's father.
"Where? I can't see him."

"You will. Later. It's a surprise."
The lights went down and the curtains opened.
There was a bumble-bee dance by the babies,
followed by a skating dance.
"It's Theresa's class next," whispered Dad.

They heard a referee's whistle and music, then all the boys and girls danced on stage in shorts and T-shirts. The children spun and threw an imaginary basketball at one another. They jumped in all directions, patting it around each other in circles.

Theresa, playing the referee,
whirled in and out through
the teams with her whistle,
until one team had won and
the dance was over.

The smallest and
happiest person
in the group leapt
the highest.
It was Steven.

The audience laughed and cheered.

Steven's mum was the only person not clapping.

She was too surprised even to speak.

"That small one with the red hair and freckles,

why, he can almost fly," said a woman in front of them.

"That's our Steven," said his father loudly.

The woman turned round.

"He can certainly jump, can't he?" she said, astonished.

Steven's mum was still watching the children bowing

on stage. Steven waved. His mother waved back.

"He'll make a fine basketball
player one day," said the
woman. "A fine player."
"Yes, I think he will," said
Steven's mum, and she smiled
proudly. "He'll make a fine
dancer too."